THE HUMAN BEHIND THE HERO

GAL GADOT
IS WONDER WOMAN®

HOT TOPICS

BY KATIE KAWA

Gareth Stevens
PUBLISHING

Please visit our website, www.garethstevens.com. For a free color catalog of all our high-quality books, call toll free 1-800-542-2595 or fax 1-877-542-2596.

Library of Congress Cataloging-in-Publication Data
Names: Kawa, Katie, author.
Title: Gal Gadot is Wonder Woman / Katie Kawa.
Description: New York : Gareth Stevens Publishing, [2020] | Series: The human behind the hero | Includes index.
Identifiers: LCCN 2019016319| ISBN 9781538248317 (pbk.) | ISBN 9781538248331 (library bound) | ISBN 9781538248324 (6 pack)
Subjects: LCSH: Gadot, Gal, 1985–Juvenile literature. | Motion picture actors and actresses–Israel–Biography–Juvenile literature. | Wonder Woman (Motion picture : 2017)–Juvenile literature. | Wonder Woman (Fictitious character)–Juvenile literature.
Classification: LCC PN2919.8.G33 K39 2020 | DDC 791.4302/8092 [B] –dc23
LC record available at https://lccn.loc.gov/2019016319

First Edition

Published in 2020 by
Gareth Stevens Publishing
111 East 14th Street, Suite 349
New York, NY 10003

Copyright © 2020 Gareth Stevens Publishing

Designer: Sarah Liddell
Editor: Katie Kawa

Photo credits: Cover, p. 1 Tinseltown/Shutterstock.com; halftone texture used throughout gn8/Shutterstock.com; comic frame used throughout KID_A/ Shutterstock.com; p. 5 Steve Granitz/Contributor/WireImage/Getty Images; pp. 7, 9 MARTIN BERNETTI/Stringer/AFP/Getty Images; p. 11 Frank Trapper/ Contributor/Corbis Entertainment/Getty Images; p. 13 Desiree Navarro/Contributor/ WireImage/Getty Images; pp. 15, 17 Victor Chavez/Contributor/WireImage/ Getty Images; p. 19 Dia Dipasupil/FilmMagic/Getty Images; p. 21 Michael Tran/ Contributor/FilmMagic/Getty Images; p. 23 TIMOTHY A. CLARY/Staff/AFP/ Getty Images; p. 25 Featureflash Photo Agency/Shutterstock.com; p. 27 Albert L. Ortega/Contributor/Getty Images Entertainment/Getty Images; p. 29 Emma McIntyre/ Staff/Getty Images Entertainment/Getty Images.

Printed in the United States of America

Some of the images in this book illustrate individuals who are models. The depictions do not imply actual situations or events.

CPSIA compliance information: Batch #CW20GS: For further information contact Gareth Stevens, New York, New York at 1-800-542-2595.

CONTENTS

A STRONG WOMAN

Saving the world isn't just for men. Women can also be heroes! Wonder Woman is a superhero who's strong, smart, and kind. Gal Gadot—the woman who's played her in *Wonder Woman* and other movies—is all of those things too.

BEHIND THE SCENES

WONDER WOMAN IS A CHARACTER IN DC COMIC BOOKS AND MOVIES. SHE FIRST APPEARED IN COMICS IN 1941. SHE ALSO GOES BY THE NAME DIANA OR DIANA PRINCE.

FAR FROM HOLLYWOOD

Gal Gadot grew up far from Hollywood. She was born in Israel on April 30, 1985. Gal was an active kid who loved dancing. She has one younger sister, and their parents taught them to always believe in themselves.

BEHIND THE SCENES

ISRAEL IS A COUNTRY IN THE MIDDLE EAST. GAL SPENDS A LOT OF TIME IN THE UNITED STATES NOW, BUT SHE OFTEN TRAVELS HOME TO ISRAEL TO SPEND TIME WITH HER FAMILY.

MISS ISRAEL

In 2004, Gal was named Miss Israel. This meant she was chosen to **represent** her country in the Miss Universe pageant. This is a **contest** women from around the world try to win by showing off their beauty and talent.

BEHIND THE SCENES

GAL DIDN'T THINK SHE WOULD WIN MISS ISRAEL, AND SHE DIDN'T WANT TO BE NAMED MISS UNIVERSE. SHE WAS HAPPY WHEN SHE LOST, AND THEN SHE STARTED STUDYING LAW IN SCHOOL.

9

A FAST RISE TO STARDOM

Gal soon started trying out for parts in movies. In 2009, she got her first big part in the movie *Fast & Furious*, playing a character named Gisele. She played Gisele in other *Fast & Furious* movies too.

BEHIND THE SCENES

IN 2010, GAL WAS IN THE MOVIES
DATE NIGHT AND KNIGHT AND DAY.
SHE WAS ALSO IN MOVIES AND ON
TV SHOWS MADE IN ISRAEL.

A SUPERHERO SECRET

The next part Gal tried out for was a secret. Gal didn't even know what it was at first! Later, she found out it was Wonder Woman. Gal got the part, and in December 2013, the world found out she was going to be Wonder Woman.

BEHIND THE SCENES

WONDER WOMAN HAD HER OWN TV SHOW IN THE 1970s. SHE WAS PLAYED BY LYNDA CARTER. LYNDA AND GAL BECAME FRIENDS AFTER GAL WAS CHOSEN TO PLAY WONDER WOMAN IN THE MOVIES.

TIME TO TRAIN!

Gal had to work hard to get

ready to play Wonder Woman.

She trained for about 8 months

and did special exercises,

such as boxing, to get in

shape to play such a powerful

superhero. Her training helped

her get very strong!

BEHIND THE SCENES

TRAINING WASN'T NEW TO GAL. IN FACT, SHE WAS AN INSTRUCTOR, OR TRAINER, IN THE ISRAEL DEFENSE FORCES (IDF), WHICH IS LIKE THE US ARMY. SHE SERVED IN THE IDF FOR 2 YEARS.

15

BATMAN V SUPERMAN

The first time fans got to see Gal as Wonder Woman was in 2016. That year, she appeared in *Batman v Superman: Dawn of Justice.* Even though Gal wasn't in the movie for very long, people loved Wonder Woman!

BEHIND THE SCENES

GAL WAS BUSY IN 2016! SHE ALSO ACTED IN THREE OTHER MOVIES THAT YEAR: *TRIPLE 9*, *CRIMINAL*, AND *KEEPING UP WITH THE JONESES*.

WORKING ON WONDER WOMAN

Gal's next movie was *Wonder Woman.* While working on it, Gal became friends with its director, Patty Jenkins. Patty was the first woman to direct a woman-led superhero movie. Gal and Patty worked hard to make a movie that would **inspire** women and girls.

REVIEW

PATTY JENKINS

ATION REVIEW

BEHIND THE SCENES

WONDER WOMAN IS FROM AN ISLAND CALLED THEMYSCIRA. ONLY WOMEN KNOWN AS THE AMAZONS LIVE ON THIS ISLAND. IN WONDER WOMAN, STRONG WOMEN WHO PLAY SPORTS PLAYED MANY OF THE AMAZONS.

19

A HIT MOVIE

Wonder Woman had never starred in her own movie before, but that changed on June 2, 2017. That's when *Wonder Woman* opened, and it became one of the biggest hits of the year. It made more than $800 million around the world!

CHRIS PINE

BEHIND THE SCENES

IN *WONDER WOMAN*, DIANA FALLS IN LOVE WITH STEVE TREVOR, WHO'S PLAYED BY CHRIS PINE. GAL AND CHRIS HAD FUN WORKING TOGETHER AND BECAME GOOD FRIENDS.

INSPIRING WOMEN

Wonder Woman meant a lot to women and girls. Gal was proud to be part of a movie that showed how strong women can be. She's a feminist, which means she believes women and men should be treated as equals.

BEHIND THE SCENES

THE MOST WELL-KNOWN PART OF WONDER WOMAN IS WHEN DIANA WALKS ACROSS NO-MAN'S-LAND AND FACES AN ARMY ON HER OWN. MANY WOMEN FELT PROUD SEEING A **FEMALE** HERO SAVE THE DAY.

23

JOINING THE JUSTICE LEAGUE

Wonder Woman is part of a group of DC heroes called the Justice League. Other Justice League members include Batman, Superman, Aquaman, the Flash, and Cyborg. The same year *Wonder Woman* came out, Gal was also part of the *Justice League* movie.

BEHIND THE SCENES

IN 2018, GAL WON THE #SEEHER AWARD. IT'S GIVEN TO ACTRESSES WHOSE WORK SHOWS WOMEN AS THEY REALLY ARE AND WHO FIGHT FOR BETTER PARTS FOR WOMEN IN MOVIES AND ON TV.

WHAT'S NEXT FOR WONDER WOMAN?

People liked *Wonder Woman* so much that a second movie about her was made soon after the first. Gal and Chris teamed up with Patty again to make *Wonder Woman 1984*. Gal said it was even more special the second time around!

BEHIND THE SCENES

GAL WAS PART OF THE DISNEY MOVIE
RALPH BREAKS THE INTERNET IN 2018. SHE
WAS THE VOICE OF SHANK, A CHARACTER
IN A RACING COMPUTER GAME.

EVERY WOMAN IS A WONDER WOMAN

Gal Gadot said her daughter likes to tell people that "every woman is a Wonder Woman." Gal's movies help people believe this is true! She inspires women around the world to believe they can be heroes just by being themselves.

BEHIND THE SCENES

AS OF 2019, GAL HAS TWO DAUGHTERS: ALMA AND MAYA. GAL WAS PREGNANT WITH MAYA WHILE MAKING PARTS OF *WONDER WOMAN*, BUT SHE DIDN'T LET THAT STOP HER FROM PLAYING A SUPERHERO.

TIMELINE

1985 GAL GADOT IS BORN ON APRIL 30.

2004 GAL IS NAMED MISS ISRAEL.

2005 GAL STARTS SERVING IN THE IDF.

2009 GAL PLAYS GISELE FOR THE FIRST TIME IN *FAST & FURIOUS*.

2010 GAL PLAYS PARTS IN *DATE NIGHT* AND *KNIGHT AND DAY*.

2013 GAL IS CAST AS WONDER WOMAN.

2016 GAL ACTS IN *BATMAN V SUPERMAN: DAWN OF JUSTICE, TRIPLE 9, CRIMINAL,* AND *KEEPING UP WITH THE JONESES*.

2017 *WONDER WOMAN* AND *JUSTICE LEAGUE* OPEN.

2018 GAL WINS THE #SEEHER AWARD, IS PART OF *RALPH BREAKS THE INTERNET,* AND FINISHES MAKING *WONDER WOMAN 1984*.

2020 *WONDER WOMAN 1984* OPENS.

FOR MORE INFORMATION

BOOKS

Duling, Kaitlyn. *Gal Gadot*. Minneapolis, MN: Jump!, Inc., 2019.

Orr, Tamra. *Gal Gadot*. Kennett Square, PA: Purple Toad Publishing, 2018.

Sherman, Jill. *Gal Gadot: Soldier, Model, Wonder Woman*. Minneapolis, MN: Lerner Publications, 2018.

WEBSITES

DC Characters
www.dccomics.com/characters
The official DC website is the place to go to learn more about Wonder Woman and the other members of the Justice League.

Gal Gadot's Official Website
www.galgadot.com/
Visitors to this website will find pictures of Gal Gadot and links to other websites she uses to connect with her fans.

IMDb: Gal Gadot
www.imdb.com/name/nm2933757/
The Internet Movie Database page about Gal Gadot has a list of all her movies and TV shows, as well as facts about her life.

GLOSSARY

award: an honor given for doing something well

contest: an event in which people try to win by doing something better than others

female: dealing with women or girls

inspire: to cause someone to want to do something great

Middle East: the area where southwestern Asia meets northeastern Africa

pregnant: carrying an unborn baby in the body

represent: to stand for

INDEX